Dear Parent:

Your child's love of reading starts here!

Every child learns to read in a different way and at his or her own speed. Some go back and forth between reading levels and read favorite books again and again. Others read through each level in order. You can help your young reader improve and become more confident by encouraging his or her own interests and abilities. From books your child reads with you to the first books he or she reads alone, there are I Can Read Books for every stage of reading:

SHARED READING
Basic language, word repetition, and whimsical illustrations, ideal for sharing with your emergent reader

BEGINNING READING
Short sentences, familiar words, and simple concepts for children eager to read on their own

READING WITH HELP
Engaging stories, longer sentences, and language play for developing readers

READING ALONE
Complex plots, challenging vocabulary, and high-interest topics for the independent reader

I Can Read Books have introduced children to the joy of reading since 1957. Featuring award-winning authors and illustrators and a fabulous cast of beloved characters, I Can Read Books set the standard for beginning readers.

A lifetime of discovery begins with the magical words "I Can Read!"

Visit www.icanread.com for information
on enriching your child's reading experience.

Pinkalicious®
and the Pinkadorable Pony

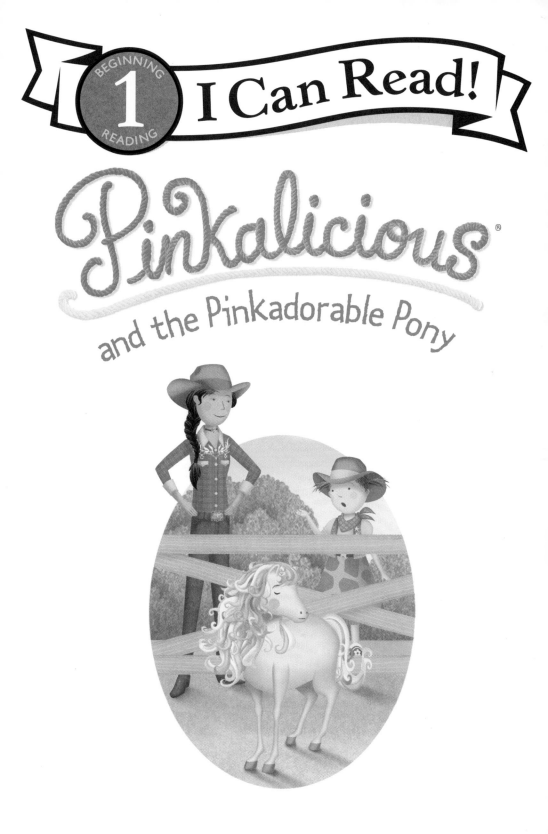

To Daia
—V.K.

The author gratefully acknowledges
the artistic and editorial contributions of
Daniel Griffo and Jacqueline Resnick.

I Can Read® and I Can Read Book® are trademarks of HarperCollins Publishers.

Pinkalicious and the Pinkadorable Pony
Copyright © 2020 by VBK, Co.

PINKALICIOUS and all related logos and characters are trademarks of Victoria Kann. Used with permission.

Based on the HarperCollins book *Pinkalicious* written by
Victoria Kann and Elizabeth Kann, illustrated by Victoria Kann
Library of Congress Control Number: 2019955940
ISBN 978-0-06-284048-6 (trade bdg.)—ISBN 978-0-06-284047-9 (pbk.)

20 21 22 23 24 LSCC 10 9 8 7 6 5 4 3 2 1
❖
First Edition

I Can Read!

Pinkalicious
and the Pinkadorable Pony

by Victoria Kann

HARPER
An Imprint of HarperCollinsPublishers

"Howdy, Pinkertons!"

a cowgirl said to my family.

"I'm Cowgirl Cassidy.

Welcome to the Pink Pines Ranch!"

"I want to ride

the most amazing horse

at the whole ranch!" I said.

Cowgirl Cassidy laughed.

"How about Flash?" she suggested.

"He's our fastest horse."

I shook my head.

"What about Polka Dot?"

Cowgirl Cassidy asked.

"She's very gentle."

I shook my head again.

The horses were all pretty,

but I wanted more.

I wanted amazing!

Suddenly I heard a cowboy yell

"WHOA!"

The cowboy was circling around
the smallest pony I'd ever seen.

"Awwww, look at the petite pony!"

"She's a miniature pony,"
Cowgirl Cassidy said.

"She doesn't have a name yet."

"I want to name her!" Peter said.

Cowgirl Cassidy laughed.

"We have a rule here," she said.

"If you train the horse,

you name the horse!

Our peewee pony

isn't trained yet," she said.

I waved at the mini-tastic pony.

"Hello, teeny, tiny pony," I said.

The pony just stared at me.

"Oh, excuse me," I said.

"You must only speak
the language of horses!"

"Neigh," I said to the pony.

"Neigh," the pony replied.

"She spoke to me!" I gasped.

"May I ride her?" I asked.

"I'm sorry, Pinkalicious,"
Cowgirl Cassidy said.
"She hasn't let anyone close enough
to ride her yet."

"You can ride Cloud instead,"
Cowgirl Cassidy told me.
Cloud was sweet,
but I couldn't stop thinking
about the itsy-bitsy pony.

Suddenly I heard another yell.

"HOLD ON, PARTNERS!"

A tall cowboy galloped over.

"The peewee pony escaped!" he said.

"Poor pony!" I said.

"Y'all split up to search for her!"

said Cowgirl Cassidy.

Mommy and I went to the hills.

"Come out, little pony!" we called.

We yelled and yelled,

but no pony came trotting over.

Then I remembered how the pony

spoke with me back in her corral.

"NEIGH!" I yelled.

"Neigh," I heard back.

"It's the pony!" Mommy gasped.

"Neigh!" I called again.

"Neigh, NEIGH!" the pony replied.

"There she is!" I said.

The little pony was up on a hill,

in the field of pink pine trees.

"Braaay!" I whinnied.

"Braaay!" the pony whinnied back.

"She likes you, Pinkalicious!"
Mommy said.

The pony walked toward me.

"Wow!" I gasped.

Her mane was pink

with soft pine needles.

"Neigh," I said to the pony.

"That means 'hello,'" I told Mommy.

The pony nuzzled my cheek.

"Let's get her home," Mommy said.

"Braaaay!" I told the pony.

"That means 'let's go!'"

The pony followed me to her corral.

"The peewee pony is safe!"

Cowgirl Cassidy cheered.

"Three yee-haws for Pinkalicious!"

The pony pranced in front of me.

"Yee-haw!" Cowgirl Cassidy said.

"It looks like the pony wants
you to ride her, Pinkalicious!"

Cowgirl Cassidy fetched her saddle.

"Giddy up!" I said.

The pony and I galloped

around her corral.

I waved at my family.

"Howdy, partners!" I said.

"Pinkalicious trained the pony!"

Peter said.

"She sure did,"

Cowgirl Cassidy said.

"That means she gets to name her!"

"I know the perfect name," I said.

"MINI!"

The pony grunted and stomped.

"I don't think she likes that,"
Peter said.

"How about Pinky?" I tried again.

"Cutie? Munchkin?"

The pony huffed and snorted.

"Hmm," I said.

"She needs a name

that's as pinkadorable as she is."

Suddenly the horse neighed

and pranced.

"She likes that!" Peter said.

I gave the tiny pony a hug.

"Meet PINKADORABLE,

the most pinkatastic, pinkerrific,

peewee pony

at Pink Pines Ranch!"